Lulu

and the Hedgehog in the Rain

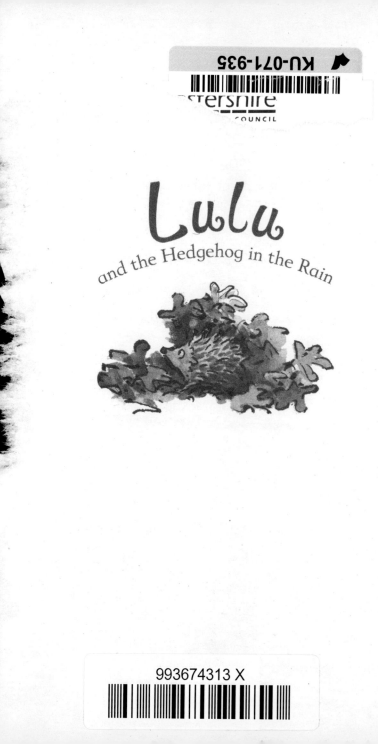

Look out for more books by

Hilary McKay

Lulu and the Duck in the Park

Lulu and the Dog from the Sea

Lulu and the Cat in the Bag

Lulu and the Rabbit next Door

www.hilarymckay.co.uk

Lulu
and the Hedgehog in the Rain

Hilary McKay

Illustrated by Priscilla Lamont

SCHOLASTIC

For Daniel Cooper.
I remembered how much your Great-Grandad liked
hedgehogs, and that gave me the idea for this story!
With love from Hilary McKay

First published in the UK in 2012 by Scholastic Children's Books
An imprint of Scholastic Ltd
Euston House, 24 Eversholt Street
London, NW1 1D, UK
Registered office: Westfield Road, Southam, Warwickshire, CV47 0RA
SCHOLASTIC and associated logos are trademarks and/or
registered trademarks of Scholastic Inc.

Text copyright © Hilary McKay, 2012
Illustrations copyright © Priscilla Lamont, 2012

The rights of Hilary McKay and Priscilla Lamont to be identified as the
author and illustrator of this work has been asserted by them.

Cover illustration © Priscilla Lamont, 2012

ISBN 978 1 407 13200 6

A CIP catalogue record for this book is available
from the British Library

Typeset by M Rules
Printed by CPI Group (UK) Ltd, Croydon, CR0 4YY

Papers used by Scholastic Children's Books are made from
wood grown in sustainable forests.

1 3 5 7 9 10 8 6 4 2

www.scholastic.co.uk/zone
www.hilarymckay.co.uk

Chapter One

The Wettest Day for Sixty-Four Years

Lulu and Mellie, who were cousins, were visiting their nan. It was an indoor visit, because of the weather.

Lulu said, "This is the wettest day of my life!"

Nan thought about that. Lulu was seven years old. In those seven years, had there ever been a day as wet as this one? No.

"You're right!" she told Lulu. "It is the wettest day of your life!" Then Nan thought a bit longer, and added, "I think

 1

it may even be the wettest day of my life too!"

"How old are you, Nan?" asked Lulu.

"Sixty four," said Nan with pride. "Sixty four, and I cannot remember a wetter day!"

"It's the driest day of my life," remarked Mellie, who was lying on the floor drawing, "because I'm not going out!"

"Wouldn't you like to, even for a minute?" asked Lulu.

"No I wouldn't!" said Mellie, and she carried on drawing her picture of a desert with palm trees and camels and other dry things. She didn't like rain, and neither did Nan, but Lulu was fascinated. She couldn't stop looking out of the window.

On that day, the wettest in sixty-four years, the rain fell from the sky in straight lines of water. In the garden the flowers were bent into puddles of brightness. The autumn leaves were washed down from the trees. The cars in the road left wakes of waves, like ships on the sea. The gutters beside the pavements bubbled like rivers.

Nan's three cats could not believe their eyes. They begged to go out and see for themselves.

"Don't be silly, cats!" said Mellie.

Lulu understood. She wanted to go out too. It seemed a waste to spend the wettest day for sixty-four years keeping dry indoors.

"I've got my wellies and my umbrella," said Lulu, who had arrived at Nan's house wearing these things earlier in the day, when the rain had just been plain rainy rain, before it had turned into a flood.

"Don't be silly, Lulu!" said Nan.

So Lulu had to watch from the window for a little longer, until Nan and Mellie went into the kitchen to do some nice dry baking.

Then, very quietly, Lulu picked up her umbrella, pulled on her wellies, opened the front door and stepped outside.

So did Nan's three cats.

One, two, three, they stepped outside.

 4

Zip!
Zip!
Zip!

They turned and fled back in again. That was enough rain for them.

It wasn't enough for Lulu. Carefully she closed the door behind the cats, and then she stood in Nan's little front garden and enjoyed the tremendous sound of a skyful of rain pounding down on her umbrella. In the road the cars flung up lace curtains of water as they passed. In the gutter, brown leaves twirled and surfboarded down to the drains. Lulu thought, This is the most fantastic weather for sixty-four years!

Then something else came tumbling down the gutter. Not surfboarding like a leaf, but rolling and bumping like a prickly grey ball.

"Oh!" gasped Lulu, when she saw what it was, and she rushed out of the garden (which she was not allowed to do) and on to the pavement. Then she splashed across to the edge of the road, bent down, and scooped the poor grey ball out of the gutter.

It was a hedgehog.

"Ouch! Ouch! Ouch!" gasped Lulu, because a hedgehog, even a small and wet one, is not a comfortable thing to hold in bare hands. Still, she held on tight, and, leaving her umbrella behind on the pavement, ran back to Nan's house. The hedgehog took two hands to hold it safe. Lulu knocked on the door with her head.

"LULU!" cried Nan.

"Look what I've got! It's a hedgehog!"

"LULU, YOU TERRIBLE CHILD!"

"Could you just hold it a minute while I fetch my umbrella?"

"LULU, GET INSIDE THIS HOUSE THIS MOMENT! GOODNESS GRACIOUS, WHAT WILL YOU DO NEXT?"

All the time Nan was saying these things she was putting on her boots, her coat, her hat, her gloves and her scarf.

 7

When they were on she rushed upstairs
and came back wearing the shower curtain
like a shawl. Then she chose her largest
umbrella, opened it and stepped bravely
outside. She was just in time to meet
Lulu coming back with her own umbrella,
rescued from the street.

"Lulu!" gasped Nan, and zipped back in
again, just like the cats had done
a few minutes earlier.

"Is it still raining?" asked
Mellie, appearing from the
kitchen. Then she looked at
Lulu and said, "Yes," and
disappeared back into the
warm again.

Water ran in streams
from Lulu's hair and face.
It trickled from
her sleeves.

It puddled around her boots.

"Lulu," said Nan. "Go upstairs and take everything off! Drop it in the bath! Put on my big pink dressing gown from the back of the bathroom door and come straight down!"

Lulu had vanished to do these things before Nan remembered something else.

"Lulu!" she called up the stairs. "Did you say A HEDGEHOG?"

"Yes, but it's all right," called back Lulu, as she dropped her jumper in the bath with a splash.

"What do you mean, all right?"

"Not dead!" shouted Lulu, squelching out of her socks.

"Have you taken it upstairs?"

"No," said Lulu, reappearing at the top of the stairs in Nan's dressing gown. "I put it on the sofa."

"ON THE SOFA!"

"Just for a few minutes, while I went back for my umbrella. It won't fall. I put cushions all around. See!"

She was downstairs again now, in Nan's tidy living room, gently lifting a green velvet cushion from Nan's silky grey sofa. There underneath was a large patch of damp and in the middle of the damp was a small curled hedgehog.

"Hmm!" said Nan. "Next time, Lulu, you think it is a good idea to leave a half drowned hedgehog on my sofa, please wrap it in a towel first."

"Sorry, Nan," said Lulu, but she could tell that Nan was not really cross. She was looking at the hedgehog very kindly. The hedgehog was trembling so hard its whole spiky little ball of a body rocked on the sofa. Every now and then, tight in its ball, it sneezed.

"Aww!" said Mellie.

They wrapped it in warm towels and took it into the kitchen and Lulu tried to remember everything she knew about hedgehogs.

"They eat cat food," she said, "and they come out at night. Perhaps they don't like brightness."

In case it didn't like brightness they found it a shoebox and put it inside, away from the light. That seemed to be a good idea. At last the trembling slowed down, and the hedgehog began to uncurl. It stuck its nose in the air and snuffled and sneezed while Lulu and Mellie and Nan watched and whispered.

"What is it sniffing?"

"Us, I suppose."

"Us!" said Mellie indignantly. "We don't smell!"

"To a hedgehog we do."

Mellie sniffed her hands. They smelt slightly of pencil sharpenings. She sniffed Nan, who smelt of coconut, and Lulu, who smelt of rain. Then, very cautiously, she sniffed the hedgehog.

"Worse than wet dogs!" said Mellie.

"I like the smell!" said Lulu, who liked everything about animals, even things that other people did not like at all.

"What are you going to do with it?"

"Take it home," said Lulu, and she sounded so surprised to be asked the question that Nan and Mellie laughed. Then Nan went away to take off her shower curtain and Mellie went back to her drawing and Lulu was left alone with her hedgehog. She leaned over the box and sniffed.

"Lovely!" she said.

At the end of the day Lulu went home with the shoebox with the hedgehog inside. She also had some cat food borrowed from Nan's cats for the hedgehog's supper; some flea powder, also borrowed from Nan's cats, for just in case; her still-damp jumper; and her wellies in a carrier bag.

Lulu dropped everything except the box just inside the door and carefully put the shoebox on the table.

"You'll never guess!" she told her parents.

"There are air holes in the box lid," said Lulu's mother, "so we might!"

"It's something we've never had before!" said Lulu very proudly.

Lulu was always appearing with animals in need of help. Stray dogs, unwanted rabbits, spare guinea pigs, noisy hamsters and goldfish-grown-out-of-their-bowls had all found happy homes at Lulu's house. A tortoise lived in the garden and a parrot lived in the sitting room. It was hard to think of anything that they had never had before.

Lulu's father said he supposed it must be a smallish armadillo.

"That's nearly right!" said Lulu, and then she took off the box lid and showed them the hedgehog she had found in the rain. They gazed, and said, "Oh, how wonderful!" and "Just as good as an armadillo!" and Lulu smiled happily.

But the hedgehog did not seem happy. It sneezed and trembled and ate nearly nothing. A lick of cat food from the end of a teaspoon, that was all.

Perhaps it got seasick, sailing down the gutter like that! thought Lulu. Seasick and bumped and frightened and cold. No wonder it wasn't hungry.

When Lulu went to bed that night, the hedgehog went too, tucked up in the box beside Lulu's pillow. And every time Lulu heard a rustle or a sneeze she thought, Good! Still alive!

All the next morning the hedgehog slept, and the sleep made it better. The sneezing stopped, and in the afternoon it woke up and ate a large late lunch. Soon it was well enough to climb out of the shoebox and go exploring in Lulu's bedroom. That was what was happening when Mellie came up the stairs.

"It looks loads better!" said Mellie.

"It is!" said Lulu proudly. "It got so much better after it had something to eat that even its fleas got better! Jumping!"

"Oh," said Mellie, backing down the stairs very quickly.

"Don't worry, we flea-powdered them," said Lulu. "Poor fleas. But I don't think the hedgehog minded. What it needs now is somewhere to live. I thought we could make it a little house in the garden."

"And we have to think of a name too," said Mellie.

"We can do both together," said Lulu,

scooping the hedgehog back into its shoebox again. "Let's start right now! Come on!"

Chapter Two

Sonic-for-Short

The house that Lulu and Mellie built for the hedgehog was at the very end of Lulu's garden, against the garden shed. The shed made one wall. Old bricks made the others. A spare roof tile was propped so it would keep out the rain. Inside they put

dry leaves and hay from the bag that Lulu kept for her rabbits and guinea pigs.

"It's a bit scruffy, though," said Mellie worriedly. "Won't the hedgehog escape without a proper door? And what about things to play with, like you give to the rabbits?"

Lulu looked at Mellie in surprise. She had not realized that Mellie thought the hedgehog was going to be a pet, with toys to play with to save it from boredom, and a proper, escape-proof door.

"This hedgehog is a wild animal," she explained. "It won't need toys or a proper door because it'll be able to go in and out whenever it likes. It'll have the whole garden."

"It doesn't seem safe," said Mellie, but when she looked around the garden she saw that it was safe. Lulu's garden had a fence all around. If the gate was closed there was no way out.

 20

"And it won't get lost," admitted Mellie, "because the garden's so little. We still need a name. What have you thought of?"

"I wondered if we should call it after Nan."

"You can't call a hedgehog Nan!" protested Mellie.

"Not Nan! Cherry! That's Nan's real name."

"Cherry's not a very hedgehoggy name!"

"What is, then?"

Mellie lifted up the shoebox lid and looked at the hedgehog.

"Pineapple," she said.

"Pineapple!"

"Or Prickles."

"Nearly every hedgehog in the world is called Prickles," objected Lulu.

There was a pause while Lulu and Mellie patted hay and leaves into a comfortable

bed and tried to think of a name that no
hedgehog in the world had yet been called.

"Bubbles!" said Lulu.

"John!" said Mellie.

"John? John! Are you mad?"

"John Cherry Bubbles Pineapple Prickles,"
said Mellie. "Five names, like the queen!"

"The queen is called Elizabeth," said
Lulu. "Come on, hedgehog! Come out
and see if you like your new house!"

She tipped the shoebox gently and the hedgehog came hurrying out at once, its blackcurrant nose twitching. In and out of the little house it went, and then off around the garden.

"Queenie," said Mellie. "John Cherry Bubbles Pineapple Prickles Elizabeth Queenie!"

Then Mellie got the giggles and had to lie on the ground.

"Crazy!" said Lulu, scattering her with autumn leaves. "Hey, Mellie, we're surrounded! Look!"

Faces had suddenly appeared: two on one side of the garden, one on the other, Lulu's neighbours peering over their fences to see what all the fuss was about. Arthur on one side, Charlie and his friend Henry, who lived a little further down the street, on the other. Lulu and Mellie knew them well. They were all in the same class at school together.

"What have you got?" asked Arthur. "Another rabbit?"

"A hedgehog!" said Lulu proudly.

"A hedgehog?" repeated Henry, and Charlie asked, "A live hedgehog? I've only ever seen squashed ones! Where?"

Lulu pointed to where the hedgehog was busy snuffling under a rabbit hutch, and all three boys at once scrambled over their fences and into the garden.

"I've always wanted to meet an actual hedgehog!" said Henry excitedly. "I don't believe they're as prickly as they look!"

"They are," said Mellie, who had said the same thing only the day before, but all three boys insisted on crawling under the rabbit hutch and testing for themselves.

"Hey Sonic!" called Arthur, while Henry reached out a fascinated, frightened finger.

"Careful!" warned Charlie.

Henry could not have been more careful if he had been about to poke a crocodile.

"It stings!" he said, wriggling backwards as fast as he could.

"Come out now before you scare it!"
said Lulu. "And it's not called Sonic either!"

"What's it called, then?" asked Arthur.

"We're still choosing," said Lulu quickly.

"Sonic's a brilliant name," said Arthur.
"Sonic the hedgehog. I've got the game
for my XBox!"

"Is it going to live here, then?" asked
Charlie.

"Yes. Wild in the garden."

"Oh, it's not fair!" burst out Henry. "I've
only got one fat boring hamster! I want a
hedgehog! Where do you get them?"

"You can't just get them," said Lulu.

"You did!"

"I found it," explained Lulu. "Washed
away in all that rain."

"What about a swop, then? You can
have my hamster!"

"No!" protested Lulu.

"My hamster and my *Tyrannosaurus rex!*"
said Henry. "It only needs new batteries!"

"No!"

"What, then?" demanded Henry, who
was used to getting his own way.

"Nothing," said Lulu. "Anyway, it's not
mine to swop. It's a wild animal! It belongs

 27

to itself. It's just living here, that's all!"

"What if it wants to live somewhere else?"

"It likes it here," said Lulu.

At first this seemed true. The hedgehog seemed happy and it soon grew used to people. Every evening, at the clink of the food plate, it came out of its house to eat up its supper, before trundling off in search of slugs and snails and wood lice and other hedgehog treats. By the time Lulu went to bed it would have vanished into the shadows. But it always came back. Some time during the night, while the humans were asleep, the hedgehog would return to the little house and put itself to bed. In the mornings, if Lulu bent very close to the little house, she could hear the magical sound of a hedgehog snoring.

"Sleep tight, Hedgehog!" she whispered.

She and Mellie still hadn't agreed on a name.

Then things began to change. The hedgehog no longer seemed quite as happy in Lulu's garden. It seemed to want to visit Charlie's as well. It found a tiny gap under the fence in between, and it would not leave it alone.

It scraped and scratched until it had quite a large hole. Almost a way through. Lulu filled the hole with stones, which made her feel even worse than flea-powdering the fleas had done.

The stones did not stop the hedgehog. Bit by bit, pushing and digging, it began working on the hole again.

Lulu and Mellie worried. They spent a whole afternoon in Lulu's bedroom, worrying and worrying.

"John Cherry Bubbles Pineapple Prickles Elizabeth Queenie Sonic-for-Short is being so silly!" said Mellie.

"It's what hedgehogs do," said Lulu.

"Be silly?"

"No! Wander! Look at this book. It tells you."

It was a book that Lulu had found in the library at school. It was a book entirely about hedgehogs. Lulu had read the whole thing, and now she knew more about hedgehogs than she ever had before.

"One garden isn't enough," she told Mellie. "Especially a little garden like ours.

It says a proper
wild hedgehog needs
much more space than
that. But if we let the
hedgehog go through
to Charlie's garden,
then what?"

"Then it'll be
lost," said Mellie.

There was a map
in the hedgehog
book. It showed the
track of a hedgehog
exploring at night.

Mellie began
drawing a map of

her own. She drew Lulu's garden and
Arthur's garden and Charlie's garden. She
drew the fences in between. Mellie drew
her lines hard and black because she was

cross. She said, "I thought we were going to look after the hedgehog."

"We are," said Lulu.

"Well then, we should fill in that hole and not let it make any more. It could have a lovely run to play in like the rabbits have. We could put in leaves and branches and things to explore. Then it would be safe."

"Then it would be a pet hedgehog, not a wild hedgehog," said Lulu. She pulled Mellie's map towards her and asked, "What comes after Charlie?"

"The New Old Lady."

"Oh yes."

Mellie took her map back and continued her drawing. She murmured as she drew.

"Arthur's garden, Lulu's garden, Charlie's garden, New Old Lady's garden. . ." (They called her the New Old Lady because she had just moved in to the street.) "Empty garden, Bossy Man's garden, Henry's garden. . ."

Mellie drew wiggly lines to show where the gardens were divided by hedges, and straight ones to show where there were fences. After Charlie's garden there were only hedges.

"See how far the hedgehog could go if it gets under the fence," said Mellie. "All the way to Henry's!"

"That's what a wild hedgehog should be able to do," said Lulu.

"It wouldn't be safe. Even going as far as Charlie's wouldn't be safe. Their gate is open all the time. It would get out on to the road."

"Not if Charlie shut it."

"How do you know the New Old Lady would care about hedgehogs?"

"How do you know she wouldn't? We could ask. We could go and talk to her."

"What, and go and talk to the Bossy Man too? I don't want to!"

Lulu didn't want to either. The Bossy Man was nearly always cross. He tried not to be, but he was. He liked peace and quiet and tidiness. It was unlucky for the Bossy Man that he lived where he did, next door to Henry. It made him bossier and crosser than ever.

"Henry is the worst of all," said Mellie. "He wants the hedgehog for himself."

"Nobody can have that," said Lulu.

"No, because it's yours."

"Not really. I'm just trying to look after it. But I can't on my own, in one little garden. What if everyone helped, you and me, and Arthur and Charlie and Henry, and the New Old Lady and

35

the Bossy Man as well. . . If we had a hedgehog club. . ."

Mellie, who had been drawing hedgehog footprints all around the edge of her map, rolled over and looked at Lulu.

"A hedgehog club?" she asked.

"Yes, for people who would keep their gardens hedgehog-safe."

"A proper club, like the *Doctor Who* club at school? They have badges. The Hedgehog Club could have badges! I could make them with my badge-making machine!"

"Do you think it's a good idea, then?"

"If I can make the badges I do."

"You can make the badges. We'll give them to everyone who says they'll help."

"Free badges for hedgehog clubbers!" said Mellie. "And I know what! Free maps of the gardens to show them how important they are! I love drawing maps!

Who'll we ask first?"

"Charlie," said Lulu at once, "because before the hedgehog can go anywhere we've got to make Charlie start shutting his gate."

Chapter Three

The Hedgehog Club

Charlie's garden had a gate that drove his family mad. It was an ordinary gate. It opened and closed like any other gate. But it was open much more than it was closed because Charlie could never remember to shut it.

Rubbish blew in and annoyed his mother. Stray dogs wandered in and bothered the cat. Once a football burglar burgled Charlie's big brother's brand new football.

"Shut the gate, Charlie!"

"Charlie! The gate!"

"Come back, please, Charlie, and. . ."

But as often as not, before they stopped speaking, Charlie would have vanished.

Late for school.

Rushing down to Henry's.

Wobbling on his skateboard.

And there would be the gate, left open again.

Getting Charlie to join the Hedgehog Club was not easy. Lulu and Mellie went around to his house after school and at first he was very stubborn.

"I don't like clubs," he said. "They've chucked me out of that *Doctor Who* one and I'm never joining any more again!"

"We won't chuck you out; we want you in!" said Lulu. "The Hedgehog Club is a brilliant club! No chucking out and free maps and badges!"

Charlie still was not happy. He looked
at his free map, and insisted on drawing
himself on it. He looked at Mellie's badges
and said, "No way! "I heart hedgehogs"!
I'm not wearing that!"

"If I make you a different badge will
you join?" asked Mellie.

"What else do I have to do?"

"Shut your gate!"

Charlie said he wasn't going to be told
what to do.

"We're not," said Mellie. "We're just
saying you've GOT to remember to shut
your gate!"

"That's telling me what to do!" said
Charlie sulkily. "Anyway, I nearly always do."

"You nearly always don't!" said Lulu.
"So Mellie's made you a special notice to
fix on it to remind you."

Mellie was good at art. Her notices were bright and bold. Charlie's said in fierce red letters:

SHUT THIS GATE!

"How bossy!" said Charlie.

"Charlie," said Lulu. "It's really important!"

When Lulu said important, Charlie's face changed. It looked interested for the first time.

Lulu and Mellie made a new notice.

Very Important!
Please Keep Charlie's Gate Shut!

And Mellie made a new badge, especially for Charlie. SHARP! NOT FLAT! said the badge she made, around a picture of a very sharply prickled hedgehog indeed.

 42

"That's better!"
said Charlie, and he
was in.

Henry was the next
person they asked.
At first he could not understand it.

"But you're letting it go!"

"Sort of."

"When you wouldn't even swop?"

"Only if we can make a hedgehog club
to keep the gardens safe."

"My garden's safe. It's got walls all
round except for the Bossy Man's side
and the gate shuts itself."

"Good."

Henry looked at his map. With his
finger he traced a line from Lulu's garden
to his.

"It could come straight to me."

"It could go anywhere," agreed Lulu.

"OK," said Henry. "I'll join! Where's my badge?"

Mellie had made him a wonderful badge. KEEP SPIKY! it said, with a picture of a hedgehog with its spikes arranged in a way that looked very like Henry's own hair.

"Cool!" said Henry.

Arthur was easy. Mellie did him all by herself when Lulu wasn't listening.

"Do you want to join our hedgehog club to help look after Sonic-for-Short?" she asked.

"Yes," said Arthur.

Arthur's badge said TEAM SONIC!

"Good name!" said Arthur.

"Sonic?" asked Lulu doubtfully, when she heard.

"Sonic-for-Short!" said Mellie.

"Oh all right!" said Lulu. "Who next?"

"I think the New Old Lady," said Mellie. "I think you should leave the Bossy Man till last!"

Lulu noticed that she said "you" and not "we".

"The New Old Lady might be even worse than the Bossy Man," she said.

"Let's ask Charlie what she's like," suggested Mellie. "He should know. He lives next door."

Charlie was helpful. He had not lived next door to the New Old Lady for long, but he knew all about her.

"She's nice," he told Lulu. "She's very nice to our family, anyway! She has to be!"

"Why?"

Charlie explained that the first thing the New Old Lady had done after coming to live next door was to reverse her car into his dad's motorbike.

"It was parked outside our house where he always puts it," said Charlie. "And she said she didn't see it! She bashed it down and then she ran over it! And then she came round all in a flap and we had to give her a cup of tea."

"But why does that make her have to be nice?" asked Lulu.

Charlie explained. His family had been nice about the motorbike. Now the New Old Lady had to be nice back. She had to throw back footballs. She had to put up with Charlie and Henry's rock band practices.

 46

"And she'll have to join the Hedgehog Club!" said Charlie. "I'll come with you to ask her if you like, to make sure."

Charlie was right. There never was a nicer old lady. She came smiling to her door to talk to Lulu and Mellie and Charlie. She loved her I HEART HEDGEHOGS badge and she said she always kept her gate locked so they needn't worry about that.

"We used to have a hedgehog in the garden when I was a girl," she told them. "Dear little things!"

"Yes they are," agreed Lulu. "And useful. Sonic-for-Short will eat up your slugs and snails for you too."

"Don't talk to me about slugs and

 47

snails!" groaned the New Old Lady. "This garden is full of the beasties! I've been putting down slug pellets. I must have killed hundreds already!"

"Oh please don't do that!" exclaimed Lulu. "What if Sonic-for-Short ate slug pellets by mistake? Or some of the poor poisoned slugs?"

"Oh, that would never happen," said the New Old Lady cheerfully. "Bread and milk! That's what hedgehogs like best! Your little hedgehog won't bother with slugs and snails if it has bread and milk for supper. It will be nice to have a hedgehog to feed again. . . Oh! Goodness! Where has she gone?"

Charlie and Mellie couldn't guess. Lulu had dashed away without a word of explanation. She returned a minute later, and flopped down panting on the doorstep.

"I went for my hedgehog book," she said, hurriedly turning pages. "Look! It tells you everything! Where they live . . . making houses . . . how to tell their footprints from cats and rabbits and things! Here's a bit about hibernation (that's when they go to sleep all winter) and here's what they eat. Slugs. Snails. Wood lice. Beetles. No bread and milk! It makes them ill! It tells you! See?"

"We always put out bread and milk," protested the New Old Lady.

"If you want to feed them you should give them cat food," said Lulu. "That's what this book says. That's what we do."

"You'd have all the local cats around," said the New Old Lady. "I don't want that! I'm not feeding cats."

"Don't you like cats?" asked Mellie.

"We've got a cat," said Charlie.

"Oh yes. I forgot." The New Old Lady sounded tired of being nice. She said, in a not-very-joking voice to Lulu, "Are you going to sit there on the doorstep and read the whole book?"

"Please would you not put out bread and milk for Sonic-for-Short, please?" begged Lulu. "And not poison the slugs and snails in your garden any more?"

50

"How else can I get rid of them?" asked the New Old Lady.

"I could come with a bucket," offered Lulu. "We all could! The Hedgehog Club! We could collect your slugs and snails and take them home. That's a good idea, isn't it?"

The New Old Lady gave up. She agreed to no bread and milk and she agreed to snail collecting and then she shut her door very quickly, as if she didn't want to have to agree to anything else.

"I told you she was nice!" said Charlie, and Lulu said, "Yes," but Mellie looked thoughtful.

"Slugs and snails in a bucket?" she asked, after a while.

"What could be easier?" asked Lulu cheerfully.

Mellie did not reply.

★

After the New Old Lady there was only the Bossy Man left.

"I can't go with you," said Mellie to Lulu. "He doesn't like me or Arthur. He moaned to our mums about the chalk pictures we drew in the street."

Charlie wouldn't go either. He had once accidentally thrown a football boot through the Bossy Man's windscreen. He wished he hadn't. The Bossy Man wished he hadn't. But neither of them could ever forget it.

"I'm not going," said Henry. "He's been complaining ever since I got my trampoline!"

"Why?"

"He says I keep appearing. Pulling faces. It's just my trampolining face!"

"'S'cos you cross your eyes," said Mellie.

"Not on purpose."

"And stick out your tongue!"

"Everyone does, jumping."

"And waggle your fingers with your thumbs in your ears!"

"Anyway, I'm not going near him," said Henry, and Arthur and Charlie and Mellie said the same, but Mellie also added something very sensible: "Ask Nan!"

Nan was the answer. She liked the Bossy Man. She liked his garden. She understood completely about chalk all over the pavement, and boots through windscreens, and trampolining neighbours with terrible faces. She and the Bossy Man talked about these things as he tidied his garden. They talked about how to prune roses too, and the way the leaves blew in from the park down the road, and how hard it had rained on the day of the hedgehog rescue. And before he knew it, the Bossy Man had joined the Hedgehog Club too.

"You needn't worry about my gate," the Bossy Man told them. "I keep it locked because of the ki. . ." He paused, looked at Lulu, and tried again. ". . .wind! Is that for me?"

Lulu nodded and handed him his badge. SONIC-FOR-SHORT RULES! Mellie had written, around a picture of a hedgehog in a crown. (The crown had been Lulu's idea. "Just right for such a bossy man," Mellie had agreed.)

The Bossy Man put his badge in his pocket with the map wrapped around it and said he would look at them both later, when he had finished raking the leaves.

"Thank you," said Lulu, and she went home with Nan very happily. Later, she went down to Sonic-for-Short's hedgehog house to whisper the news.

"We've made you a Hedgehog Club, so you can be a wild hedgehog! You can go as far as you want to now. All the gardens are safe."

"Brrrr!" went Sonic-for-Short's tiny snore.

There was one star out in a purple sky. There was the cheerful sound of voices coming from the park. There was a lovely smell of damp grass and bonfire smoke in the air.

Bonfire smoke! thought Lulu, and she remembered the Bossy Man's pile of raked-up leaves. Then she leapt to her feet and ran.

"What? What?" demanded the Bossy Man as she hurtled down his garden path.

"You can't have bonfires!" shouted Lulu.

"WHAT?"

"You might cook a hedgehog!"

"WHAT?" said the Bossy Man.

"They hide in piles of leaves just like that!"

"Remind me of your name!" said the Bossy Man.

"Lulu."

"Lulu, there is no hedgehog in this pile of leaves. I know. I raked them up myself, only this afternoon. You were here. You saw me."

"I didn't see you rake up the whole pile."

"Well, I did."

"All of it this afternoon?"

 56

"Nearly."

"Was there a little pile to start with?"

"Yes, but there was no hedgehog in the little pile."

"Did you check?"

"Not under every leaf," admitted the Bossy Man, and he began to put out his bonfire, raking and stamping until he was left with nothing but great piles of smoky damp leaves all over his garden.

"What am I to do with them?" he grumbled.

"Couldn't you just leave them on the grass?"

"Certainly not!"

"Or put them in the bin?"

"Not allowed!"

"They blew here. Perhaps they will blow away again."

"I don't think so."

"You know the New Old Lady?" asked Lulu.

"No."

"The one who squashed up Charlie's dad's motorbike."

"Go on!"

"The Hedgehog Club are taking away her slugs and snails so she doesn't use poisonous slug pellets. Would you like us to take away your leaves as well?"

"Where to?"

"My garden. In the wheelbarrow. It would be easy!"

"Are the slugs and snails going there too?"

Lulu nodded.

"What do your parents say about that?"

"They don't mind," said Lulu cheerfully. "I take home all sorts of things. They never mind. Even when I took home four rabbits

 58

all in one go they didn't. I'm always looking for new things for my rabbits to play with. They'd love your leaves!"

The Bossy Man stood thinking for a very long time.

"All right," he said at last. "You take my leaves for your rabbits. I'll give up the bonfires. We'll see how it goes."

"The Bossy Man is giving me all his leaves for my rabbits," Lulu told her father as she brushed the dogs that night.

"All of them?" asked her father. "All of them! All those great heaps that blow in from the park?"

"Yes. It's so he doesn't have to burn them in a bonfire. It's a Hedgehog Club thing."

Lulu's father groaned and her mother asked, "Are there any more Hedgehog Club things we should know about?"

 59

"There's closing the gates," said
Lulu, ticking them off on her
fingers. "But we always do because of
the dogs. Not having bonfires. No giving
them bread and milk because it makes
them sick. And the New Old Lady's slugs
and snails. Poor little things."

"Why are they poor little things?" asked
Lulu's mother.

"Because she's been feeding them poisonous slug pellets," said Lulu. "She's killed hundreds! She told me! But she's not killing any more. They're coming here to live instead. The Hedgehog Club are going to collect them everyday."

"Oh are they?" said Lulu's mother. "Well, please don't show them to me when you bring them home. It all seems a lot of work for one small hedgehog. Are you sure Mellie and the boys will help?"

"They'll love to," said Lulu.

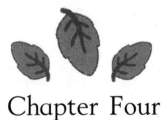

Chapter Four

Autumn

After school was a busy time at Lulu's house. There was homework to do, the two dogs to play with, and the rabbits and guinea pigs to feed. There was a tortoise whose old brown shell needed polishing with olive oil, and a parrot to be sprayed with a mist sprayer to remind him of long-ago African rains. And now there were slugs and snails to collect and gates to check and leaves to wheel in barrow loads from the Bossy Man's house.

There was a tunnel now under the fence to Charlie's garden, and another on the other side, dug by Arthur and his father. That was nice of Arthur's father, who had just put a new fence all around his garden.

"He likes hedgehogs," said Arthur. "And he said to tell you not to forget the pond in the empty garden. He says it should have a ramp so that if Sonic-for-Short falls in he can get out again, and he said to let him know if you want a hand making one."

The pond was something Lulu had forgotten, and she was very glad Arthur's father had remembered it. She helped Arthur and his father make a ramp out of a spare bit of wood and an old rubber doormat cut into strips and all three of them crept into the empty-house garden to put it into place.

"How do hedgehogs survive in the wild?" asked Lulu's father. "With no one to feed them cat food and collect them slugs and snails and rescue them from bonfires and make them houses and ramps and tunnels? Not to mention the leaves! How many more thousand tons of leaves do you think will fit into this garden?"

"Are you really cross?" Lulu asked him.

"Am I ever really cross?"

"No," said Lulu.

At night, when Sonic-for-Short came out, every moment of trouble was worth it. Lulu smiled with happiness as he rustled through the dry leaves and explored under the ivy. Slowly, slowly the hedgehog, a little round shape in the evening shadows, made his way to the gap under the fence.

Then, suddenly, he was gone.

"He'll be quite safe," said Lulu, to comfort herself. "He's being a wild hedgehog. He's doing what hedgehogs do."

All the same, in the night Lulu often woke up to stare out of her bedroom window, wondering. And in the mornings she could not wait to race out into the garden.

Had Sonic-for-Short come home?

Would there be snoring or not?

Snoring!

There was definitely snoring.

"He came home safe! He came home safe!" called Lulu to her parents at breakfast, to Nan down the phone, to Mellie and the boys on the way to school. "We let him go and he came home safe!"

Day after day Sonic-for-Short came home safe.

"It's working!" said Lulu. She was so pleased that she didn't care how many leaves she wheeled away from the Bossy Man's garden. She didn't mind how many slugs and snails she collected from the New Old Lady. She didn't mind how grumpy Charlie became when she reminded him to close his gate. She didn't even mind that Henry was being suddenly mysterious.

"I can't help with the leaves," he told Lulu and Mellie, "or the slugs and snails. I'm busy. So's Charlie. Hedgehog stuff. Soz!"

"Soz!" said Mellie, staring. "Soz! Did you say soz?"

"Yeah, soz!" said Henry. "I'll show you when it's finished!"

Henry swaggered away with his hands in his pockets. With his spiky hair and his puffy jacket and his little short legs he looked so like a hedgehog himself that

Lulu could not stop laughing.

"Soz!" said Mellie again. "Henry is just not cool enough to say soz! And what is he going to show us?"

They found out the next day. A hedgehog house. A hedgehog house in Henry's garden.

"A luxury hedgehog house!" said Henry proudly.

All Henry's family had helped to make it. Henry's father was a carpenter; there were lots of spare pieces of wood stacked behind Henry's shed. Henry's mother had given him her old kitchen blind for a roof. It had a pattern all over of bunches of grapes. Henry's grandma found him a fluffy purple bath mat to use for a carpet, and a matching purple towel for a hedgehog bed. Even Henry's hamster was useful. Hamster treats were heaped in a corner.

"They were my idea," said Charlie.

"It's a palace!" said Lulu.

"Fantastic!" said Arthur.

"Very purple," said Mellie.

"I like purple," said Henry. "But the best thing about this hedgehog house is, anytime I want to know if anyone's inside I can just take off the roof!"

Henry took off the roof to show them.

"I wouldn't like that," said Lulu, "if I was at home asleep in bed and a giant came and took the roof off to see if I was in!"

"I'd love it," said Henry, and he took off the roof several times a day.

Sometimes Charlie's cat Suzy was inside.

"See!" said Henry. "Animals like it!"

Suzy had been very pleased to discover a private purple den, with hamster treats inside, but she hated having the roof taken off. She rocketed away at the sound of Henry's footsteps.

"If Sonic-for-Short comes to live here you won't keep taking the roof on and off, will you?" asked Lulu anxiously.

"Only very carefully," said Henry.

Without meaning to, the Hedgehog Club had divided into different jobs for different people. Arthur checked the pond ramp. Charlie closed his gate. Henry added luxury extras (like doormats and a chimney) to his purple palace. Lulu and Mellie collected leaves and slugs and snails.

"We do the most," said Mellie. "Unless you count Arthur's XBox," she added enviously. The boys counted playing *Sonic the Hedgehog* on Arthur's XBox as Hedgehog Club work. They did it every day after school.

"Lucky things," said Mellie.

The leaves did not take long, but the slugs and snails took ages, especially the way Mellie collected them. Mellie did not like touching slugs and snails. She picked them up with a spoon.

"Forty-six, forty-seven, forty-eight. . ." counted Lulu, as she dropped snails into her snail-collecting bucket.

"Two, ugh! Three. . ." counted Mellie. "Lulu, Lulu, help! They're climbing up the sides of the bucket again!"

The New Old Lady covered her eyes at
the sight of Lulu's bucket and said, "You
are very brave girls!"

"You won't forget about no bread and
milk?" Lulu reminded her.

"No, but it does seem ridiculous!"
said the New Old Lady. "Our hedgehogs
always ate bread and milk."

"Shall I fetch my library book again?"

"No, no, no!" said the New Old Lady
hastily, and hurried indoors.

Every evening now, Sonic-for-Short set off on his trip around the gardens. He explored them all. In Arthur's he posed for photographs. At Charlie's he met Suzy, who jumped backwards, bristling in horror. In the New Old Lady's he was dazzled by torchlight, as the New Old Lady inspected her visitor.

"He's very small," she said to Lulu the next day. "Ours was twice the size!"

"What happened to yours?" asked Lulu.

"Oh, vanished, like they do," said the New Old Lady. Lulu patted her hand and did not say what she thought.

"I've seen her several times," said the Bossy Man, when Lulu visited to collect his leaves. "Are you sure you want all this rubbish for those rabbits?"

 74

"Oh yes!" said Lulu.

"I've been pruning as well. There's a great pile of sticks."

"Rabbits like sticks to bite on," said Lulu. "It's good for their teeth. I can take them too if you like."

★

Henry hadn't seen Sonic-for-Short in his garden, but that was not surprising. He never seemed to see anything until he walked right into it. He had stopped putting hamster treats in his hedgehog house because Suzy ate them.

"Suzy eats anything except cat food," said Charlie proudly. "Ice cream, jam, chips and cheese!"

Henry heaved the roof of his hedgehog house and peered inside.

"Still no hedgehog," he complained.

"He does come to your garden, though," said Lulu.

"How do you know?"

"Hedgehog poo," said Lulu. "Look! All under your trampoline!"

"What! That's revolting!"

"I thought you'd be pleased!"

 76

"Why did you show me? Now every time I jump I'll be thinking about poo!"

"I thought you wanted Sonic-for-Short in your garden!"

"I do! I just don't want poo!"

Henry gave another disgusted look at his trampoline, and said, "Anyone who likes can borrow it!" stomping off to his shed. He came out again carrying his skateboard.

"I'm a bit fed up of this Hedgehog Club," Lulu overheard him complaining to Charlie later that afternoon. "Poo everywhere!"

"I'm fed up of being moaned at about our gate," Charlie replied. "The second Lulu hears it squeak she comes roaring round like a tiger!"

"I thought you'd started climbing over it."

"I have, but it's no good with a bike. . ."

★

"The boys have stopped wearing their Hedgehog Club badges," Lulu said to Mellie a few mornings later.

Mellie, who wasn't wearing hers, looked guilty.

"And the Bossy Man never did. He just put it in his pocket."

"Nan wears the one we made for her," said Mellie.

"That's because she's Nan, not because of the Hedgehog Club," said Lulu. "She wears it like she wore those pasta earrings we made her. And the conker necklace, and the scarf you wove her out of bits of socks."

"Nan loved that scarf!" said Mellie. "I made it specially on that weaving thing she gave me. I don't know why everyone laughed at it."

"They didn't."

 78

"You did."

"Only because I recognized the socks."
Mellie sniffed.

"What's the matter?"

"I've got a cold," said Mellie. "And. . ."

There was a pause while Mellie waited
for Lulu to ask And what?

Lulu didn't.

The pause became longer.

"Slugs and snails!" said Mellie suddenly.

"What about them?"

"Picking them up with spoons!"

"Mellie?"

"Every day after school I think 'Oh
good! I can go home!' and then I think,
'Oh no! I can't. I've got to go and pick
up slugs and snails with spoons!'"

"I thought you liked it!"

"OF COURSE I DON'T LIKE IT!"
shouted Mellie.

 79

"Oh."

"And now I've got this cold and I don't think it would be good for me."

"It would! Fresh air!"

"I don't want fresh air," growled Mellie. "I want to go home and watch telly!"

Lulu became a Hedgehog Club on her own.

 80

It was true that Nan wore her badge whenever she came to visit.

The New Old Lady smiled and asked for Hedgehog Club news.

The Bossy Man resisted the great temptation to light bonfires.

Charlie continued to climb over his gate.

Mellie asked, almost every day, "How's Sonic-for-Short?"

Henry still looked carefully under his trampoline before he bounced on it.

Arthur began to save up for *Sonic the Hedgehog 2*.

But that was as hedgehoggy as they got.

Leaf collecting, slug-and-snail hunting, and washing up the empty cat-food saucers were left to Lulu alone. The nights got darker and slugs and snails became harder to find. The pile of the Bossy Man's leaves and sticks in Lulu's garden grew enormous. Lulu's father looked at them unhappily. Lulu's rabbits did not look at them at all. The New Old Lady hinted more than once that warm bread and milk would be just the thing for a small cold hedgehog these chilly evenings.

And then Sonic-for-Short vanished.

Chapter Five

Winter

When?

Lulu did not know. There were two days of wind, when no one could have heard an elephant snore, never mind a small hedgehog. And then the wind was mixed with icy rain, so cold it was nearly snow. And in the middle of all this weather Lulu became ill. Her throat hurt and her eyes were sore and she ached all over, and then she began to sneeze and sneeze. So she was put to bed with ice cream and tissues and terrible yellow medicine from the doctor. And Mellie was kept out of the way, in case she caught it too.

While Lulu was ill she could not look after her pets. The tortoise was asleep for the winter, in a box of hay, but the rabbits and the parrot, the guinea pigs, and the two bouncy dogs all had to manage without her. Her parents looked after them instead.

"And Sonic-for-Short too?" croaked Lulu when she was well enough to speak.

Her mother and father looked at each other, and then rushed outside with double helping of cat food and left it by Sonic-for-Short's house.

"Was there snoring?" croaked Lulu.

"What?"

"If you bend right down next to his house you can hear him snoring."

"Lulu, do you know it is nearly snowing out there?"

"Is it?"

"Sleeting and howling!"

"Can I go and see?"

"NO!" said Lulu's mother and father, but Nan, who had come over to see how the invalid was, actually picked her way down to the end of the garden and bent down to the hedgehog house and listened.

She was a good nan.

"I think I may have heard something," she told Lulu. "It was hard to tell, but I think I might!"

In the morning I can see if the cat food has been eaten, thought Lulu as she lay in bed that night.

In the morning the cat food looked like terrible half frozen soup. Hungry birds had found it and left dozens of footprints in the icy mud. It was impossible to tell whether a hedgehog had been there too.

"When can Mellie come and see me?" asked Lulu in despair.

"Poor Mellie's got this as well, now! Try and eat your soup!"

Lulu ate her soup. She swallowed her medicine. She tried so hard not to cough she nearly exploded.

"I'm better!" she announced, long

before she really felt like doing anything but lying on the sofa, and before anyone could stop her she wobbled outside.

She couldn't hear snoring.

The latest saucer of cat food had not been touched.

How long had it been since she had last seen Sonic-for-Short?

More than a week!

Had Charlie's gate been left open any time in that week?

"Are you still going on about that?" asked Charlie grumpily.

"Yes."

"I didn't leave it open. I suppose it might have blown open."

"Did it blow open?"

"It might have. A bit."

★

Lulu checked the pond in the empty garden. The ramp had half sunk and was covered in slippery fallen leaves.

"You forgot about Sonic-for-Short!" said Lulu to Arthur.

"Forgot!" said Arthur. "Forgot! Do you

know I spent nearly all my birthday money on *Sonic the Hedgehog 2*!"

"I didn't forget her!" said the New Old Lady proudly. "But I thought you'd lost interest in the poor little thing!"

Lulu shook her head.

"Anyway, I remembered!" said the New Old Lady. She sounded pleased about something. She sounded like someone who was about to explain they had been right all along.

She did.

"Every night this week I've put out a nice large plate of bread and milk!" she told Lulu. "And every morning it has all disappeared! So what do you think of that?"

The Bossy Man was just as bad.

"Bonfires?" he asked. "You think I've been making bonfires in this weather? I

89

shovelled up the last lot of garden stuff and put it in the bin."

"I thought you said the bin men wouldn't take it," said Lulu.

"I bought them some beer," said the Bossy Man. "Then they did."

"Oh," said Lulu, and then she said, "I think the hedgehog is lost."

"Ah," said the Bossy Man. "A pity."

"You couldn't have shovelled him up with your rubbish?"

"No," said the Bossy Man.

"Are you sure?"

"Absolutely. Almost absolutely."

"Almost?"

"Yes, almost."

No hedgehog ate the saucers of cat food any more. No small round shape hurried out into the dusk. One evening, the

New Old Lady discovered Suzy the cat gobbling bread and milk.

"Was it you all the time?" cried the New Old Lady.

Suzy licked her milky jaws and smiled.

"Shoo!" cried the New Old Lady crossly. "I'm not feeding cats!"

So that was that.

★

Still Lulu did not give up. One morning, when the air was so still and frosty you could hear the leaves as they fell one by one from the trees, she spent a long time listening beside the hedgehog house.

Mellie found her there.

"It's nearly tumbled down," Mellie said, looking at the little house. "If you didn't know what it was, you wouldn't know what it was! Can you hear anything?"

"I'm not sure," said Lulu. "Perhaps hedgehogs don't always snore. Perhaps sometimes they just do very quiet breathing."

"Couldn't you reach inside and see if you could feel him?"

"No! Because what if I woke him up? You shouldn't wake up hibernating animals. Sometimes they can't go to sleep again. Then they die."

"Anyway, I don't think he's there," said Mellie, after bending down to listen for herself. "I can't hear a thing. And where else could he be?"

Lulu didn't answer, but she thought of the Bossy Man's bin-bagged leaves. She thought of the pond with the ramp out of place and she thought of Charlie's gate.

But also she remembered Henry's purple palace.

Perhaps, perhaps, perhaps, thought Lulu, Sonic-for-Short was safely tucked up in Henry's purple palace.

Chapter Six

Spring

One day Lulu's two bouncy dogs bounced on the nearly tumbled-down hedgehog house and it collapsed completely. There was no hedgehog inside.

Mellie hugged Lulu and did not say, I told you so.

Lulu thought, It might still be all right. There is still Henry's.

She did not dare say this thought out loud. She didn't want Henry taking off the roof of the palace to check. She just hoped.

★

Lulu hoped all winter. All through the exciting days coming up to Christmas. All through the dark of January. All through the snow that followed. All through the long wet thaw.

Everyone else forgot the hedgehog, but Lulu kept waiting and hoping until spring.

One day in early spring Lulu's father took a long look at his garden and he said, "It's the worst in the street!"

It was. Several horrible-looking cat-food saucers. The Bossy Man's sticks, all blown about. The Bossy Man's leaves, a great dark slimy heap. The hedgehog house all tumbled down.

"Time to tidy up!" said Lulu's father.

The saucers were washed.

The sticks were gathered.

 96

A roll of garden bin bags appeared, and a shovel and a rake.

"The Bossy Man said if you give the bin men beer they will take it away," said Lulu.

"I don't think I could afford all the beer they would want to take this," said Lulu's father. "I'll drive it down to the tip."

He shovelled for ages while Lulu and Mellie held open the bags and raked the scattered leaves back into heaps. While they were busy Arthur and Charlie and Henry arrived.

Then at last Lulu said what she had been hoping all winter.

"Do you think Sonic-for-Short could be at your garden, Henry?"

"Who?" asked Henry, staring. "Oh, I remember! No."

"Not in that house you made?"

"Definitely not!"

"Are you sure?"

"Course I'm sure," said Henry. "Me and Charlie took that house to pieces ages ago to make jumps for our skateboard park."

Then everybody saw Lulu's face.

Lulu's father took charge. He got the boys out of the way by making them help him carry the filled-up bags up to his car. He gave Mellie the shovel and Lulu a hug and said, "You two rake up those last few leaves! I'll take it all away and come back by the pizza place. We'll have a pizza party because . . . because. . . Help me out here, Mellie! Why do we need a party just now?"

An early bee flew across the garden.

"Because it's spring," said Mellie, and she began to hurry with her raking, to get the job done.

But Lulu watched the bee. She watched the bee, and sniffed a lot and rubbed her eyes, and felt a warmth in the sunshine that she hadn't felt for months, and then she heard Mellie say, "Lulu!"

"I'm all right," said Lulu. "I'm not crying if that's what you thi—"

"No! No! Lulu, look! First I thought it was an old brush or something. . . Lulu, PLEASE look!"

So Lulu gave one last sniff and one last rub and turned to look and it was Sonic-for-Short.

Under the last of the leaves,
deep in a hollow, as if he had
melted into the ground.

Sonic-for-Short.

And they could see him
breathing.

Lulu and Mellie fell to their knees.
They stared. They thought of the winter
that the hedgehog had survived. Winds
so strong they blew Charlie off his bike.

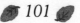

Christmas all alone. Freezing cold and frost and snow.

They fetched the boys, and the New Old Lady, and the Bossy Man. They telephoned Nan.

"Wonderful!" said Nan.

"Excellent!" said the Bossy Man.

"Amazing!" said the New Old Lady. "They usually disappear!"

Lulu thought of the times to come. More snail collecting, more worrying, more battles. Then she looked up and she thought, Perhaps not so many battles.

The Hedgehog Club was back in action.

Charlie had run to close his gate.

Arthur had dashed away to check the ramp in the pond.

Henry was staggering back from the car with a sack of leaves. The Bossy Man helped him to tip them out. Mellie and the New Old Lady began sorting out the driest.

Gently Lulu began to tuck up the sleeping hedgehog with handfuls of leaves.

The boys fetched a second bag, and then a third. They piled them around her. Then they told each other *Shush*! and tiptoed away.

And after that the Hedgehog Club had a pizza party, because it was spring!

Look out for more

Lulu

adventures
OUT NOW!